HIGHWAY ROBBERY

HIGHWAY ROBBERY

—Kate Thompson—

Illustrated by Jonny Duddle and Robert Dress

GREENWILLOW BOOKS
An Imprint of HarperCollins Publishers

Highway Robbery
Copyright © 2008 by Kate Thompson

First published in 2008 in Great Britain by The Bodley Head,
an imprint of Random House Children's Books.
First published in 2009 in the United States by Greenwillow Books.

The right of Kate Thompson to be identified as the author of this work has been asserted by her.

The text of this book is set in Bembo.
Book design by Victoria Jamieson

Library of Congress Cataloging-in-Publication Data

Thompson, Kate, (date).
Highway robbery / by Kate Thompson.
p. cm.
"Greenwillow Books."
Summary: On a cold day in eighteenth-century England, a poor young boy agrees to watch a stranger's fine horse for a golden guinea but soon finds himself in a difficult situation when the king's guard appears and wants to use him as bait in their pursuit of a notorious highwayman.
ISBN 978-0-06-173034-4 (trade bdg.)
ISBN 978-0-06-173035-1 (lib. bdg.)
[1. Adventure and adventurers—Fiction. 2. Horses—Fiction. 3. Turpin, Richard, 1706-1739—Fiction. 4. Robbers and outlaws—Fiction. 5. Great Britain—History—18th century—Fiction.] I. Title.
PZ7.T3715965Hig 2009 [Fic]—dc22 2008027720

09 10 11 12 13 CG/RRDB First Edition 10 9 8 7 6 5 4 3 2 1

 Greenwillow Books

To my wonderful neighbors,
Peter and Ann

HIGHWAY
ROBBERY

CHAPTER ONE

There are good things and bad things about being small. You wouldn't know about that, though, would you, sir? Fine, tall gentleman like yourself. But it's true. One good thing is that people often mistake me for being much younger than I am, and that makes them take pity on me. Especially the women, the ones that have their own children at home. And especially the poor ones, who know that there isn't much keeping their own little ones from begging in the streets like me. Not that I'm begging now, sir. I wouldn't want you to think that, not for a minute.

I had a change in my fortunes, sir, you see. You might not know it from looking at me—not yet, anyway. But it's true all the same. And if I hadn't been so small, it would never have happened.

You see, one of the bad things about being small is that most of the other beggar lads on the streets are bigger. And if you're bigger, you can throw your weight around, so to speak. You can choose the best place to beg and no one's going to bother you, provided you don't annoy the shopkeepers and scare off their customers. But if you're small, it's different. Whenever I found a good spot I was always chased off by some bigger lad, and many's the bruise I've had to show for it, you can take my word on that. One fellow hit me so hard, I couldn't hear anything for a week. But that was some time ago, sir, and I can hear as well as anyone now.

Why I'm telling you this is by way of explanation for how I ended up begging so far from the center of the city. I was way out on the outskirts on the day my luck changed. It was a cold, miserable day that couldn't decide whether it wanted to rain or snow. I had a pair of boots once, but they were so often wet that the nails came through and it was like trying to walk on a pair of hedgehogs, and that's the truth, sir. I let another lad steal them off me just for the pleasure of hearing him howl when he put them on.

But on that day, on the edge of the city, I had no boots and my feet were as cold as

ice and my hands were not much better.
I was hungry too, but then I'm used to
that. I do remember a time when I wasn't
hungry, sir, but it was only for a very short
time and it was a very long time ago.
There wasn't much traffic through that
street, either. It was one of those nasty,
muddy little streets, all pigs and gardyloo,
which carts avoid because they're always
getting stuck. There were a few people
walking, but no one who came along had

a coin or a crust of bread to spare, so all in all it looked as if it was going to be a very bad day for me. But then, in the blink of an eye, my luck changed.

I heard him before I saw him. I heard him through my stone-cold feet first, and then I heard him through the air, and he was like a distant storm approaching, so I couldn't tell what I was hearing. Then the sound grew nearer and clearer. It was galloping hooves, clattering through muck and ice.

Round the corner he came, a tall rider on a big black horse, and the pigs and chickens cleared the road in double-quick time to get out of his way. I stepped back myself, sir, even though I was already well out of the road, and I squeezed myself tight against the wall. Still he came on, at full tilt, his black cloak streaming in the air behind him, and now I could see his face, his cheeks red from the cold and his mustaches as black as the black horse under him.

He didn't look at me at all as he came on, but I saw his eye fix on something beside me. The alleyway, I think it was. And just as he drew level, he straightened in the saddle and reined in the

mare so fast, she sat right down on her tail in a shower of mud. Some of it hit me in the face, sir. That's how close I was.

The rider sprang off as light as a cat and pulled the reins over the horse's head. Then he marched straight over to me and put them into my hand. I gaped up at him and my mouth must have been as big as a badger hole. You can imagine, I'm sure, how astonished I was. He was very tall, that man, and his cheeks were red and he was breathing hard and there were tear tracks across his face. He looked wild and mad, sir, and I have to admit that the sight of him terrified me.

But of course, the way he looked was not because he was angry or excited but because he had been traveling so fast through the icy weather. And indeed, when he opened his mouth, it was not to yell at me, which is what I expected, but to say, quite gently: "Hold the mare for me, lad. And when I come back, I'll give you a golden guinea." And he ruffled my hair for me, sir. Look. Like this. Made it stand up like a bunch of straw. I would have done anything for him after that. I don't often meet with kindness, as I'm sure you can imagine. So I clutched tight to those reins and I closed my badger-hole mouth and I nodded my head until my teeth rattled.

"You can rely on me, sir," I said. "I won't move an inch from here until you come back."

"Good lad," he said. He pulled a saddlebag from the horse's withers, then unfastened his cloak and laid it carefully over her back. That will tell you, sir, how much value he set on his mare, because it was a cold day for a gentleman to be out and about in his shirtsleeves. He patted her on the neck, winked at me, and then he was gone, slipping away down the alley and out of sight.

CHAPTER TWO

I was as hungry as a sow with ten piglets, but I was full of satisfaction. I don't know if that makes sense, but sometimes a bit of kindness goes further than a meat pie. And to be trusted too. To be given a bit of responsibility. That can make you feel like a man even if you're only as high as a man's elbow.

And that horse, sir. I don't think I'd actually ever held one before that. Most horses I see are pulling carts, and they don't need anyone to hold them. If the driver gets down to make a delivery or to go for a pint of ale, those carthorses just wait there until he comes back. And as for carriage horses, the footmen won't let the likes of me anywhere near them. I don't know why. Maybe they're afraid I'd give them fleas or something. But there I was, holding this horse, and she was huge! Sixteen hands if she was an inch. And so beautiful. Her nostrils were red as cornfield poppies. Her eyes were wide and bright with the excitement of the gallop and she kept looking this way and that, as though she was still seeing the countryside speeding past.

I was, I have to admit, a little afraid of

her. She was so massive and hot, all covered with mud and steaming like a dragon that could burst into a fit of violence at any moment. And she was very restless to begin with because she had been ridden so hard and so fast. In that way, I suppose a horse is pretty much like a man. They neither of them can shut down their feelings as quick as they'd like to. So the mare was looking from side to side and moving from foot to foot, and then she planted her four feet out wide and shook herself so hard that the saddle flaps rattled and the black cloak slipped sideways. But for all her restlessness, she never once tried to break away from me. She didn't even pull on the reins. A pure-hearted lady through and through, sir, if ever there was one.

And as she calmed down, I became more confident, until finally I found the courage to reach up and run my fingers down the front of her nose. She let out an enormous sigh and dropped her head.

I could reach it better now, and I stroked her forehead and combed her black forelock with my fingers. I swear she liked it, and I wondered whether horses were like boys, and whether they too felt the need for a bit of kindness now and again.

So holding her was easy, but there was something that made it better than easy and turned it into a pleasure. The mare, as you would expect, was blowing hard, and her hot breath was coming straight at me and warming my miserable hands and feet. For a long time I just stood and soaked up the heat, and gradually my stony hands and feet came back to life.

But nothing lasts forever. In time the mare's breathing returned to normal, and

the cold made itself felt in my bones again.
I began to wonder when
the gentleman might
be coming back and
when I might be
setting eyes on my
golden guinea. I had
never seen one before,
and I tried to imagine
what I might do with it. I thought about
hot pies and pigs' trotters and apples and
pease pudding. I thought about the
marketplace where you could buy hand-
me-down boots for a shilling and patched
woolen blankets for sixpence. And I was
thinking so hard about hot bread that I
began to imagine I could smell it. And

then I realized that I wasn't imagining it, after all. I really *could* smell it, and I could see it as well, in the hands of two young girls who were walking along the side of the road toward me.

CHAPTER THREE

"What are you doing?" asked the taller of the two. She had a pigtail, and her skirt had a black band along the bottom where the hem had been let down.

"I'm holding this horse for a gentleman," I said.

"What gentleman?" she said.

"A gentleman," I said, "who doesn't choose to give his name to little girls."

"I'm bigger than you are," she said.

This was true, but it was also irrelevant, so I didn't answer.

"Anyway," she went on, "there aren't any gentlemen around here."

I didn't answer that, either. They stood and watched me. I watched the horse and didn't look at them, though I couldn't help stealing the occasional glance at their penny loaves. They had one each, and they were hardly even nibbled. I don't mind telling you, sir, the smell made me feel faint with hunger.

"Why is he wearing a coat?" said the smaller girl, after a while. She had a bad squint and I couldn't tell whether she was looking at me or at the horse. She might have been looking at both of us at the same time.

"It's not a he," I said. "And she's wearing a coat because she's the most valuable horse in England and she needs to be kept warm. When she's at home in her stable, she wears a felt bonnet and a silk gown, and she eats plum duff and oranges."

Squint giggled. "No she doesn't."

"And figs," I added. "She's particularly fond of figs."

She was edging closer. If it hadn't been for the horse, I could have snatched her penny loaf and run for it. I came up with another way of getting it.

"In fact," I said, "this horse is so special that it's costing me a shilling for every hour I'm allowed to hold her."

I stroked the mare's nose and she dropped her head to me again.

"I don't believe you," said Pigtail. "I never heard of anyone paying just to hold a muddy old horse."

"She may be muddy," I said, "but that doesn't mean she isn't special. Did you ever see a horse in a cloak before?"

Squint was right beside me now, reaching out timidly toward the mare's nose. I elbowed her aside.

"Look," I said, "if you're really so keen to touch Her Grace, it might be arranged. But it will cost you."

A minute later I was cramming the first of the penny loaves into my mouth and the other one into the poacher's pocket stitched inside my patched old coat. The two girls swarmed over the mare, oohing and aahing, stroking her nose and her neck, putting little plaits into her mane and tail, and doing a really good job of straightening the cloak on her back so that it hung down exactly the same amount on each side. The mare was very patient with all the attention, sir. I'd swear she knew what was going on, because she arched her neck and fluttered her eyelashes, and with all the grooming she was getting she actually began to look like royalty. But after a while I could see that she was starting to get restless, so as soon as I had swallowed the last of my loaf I told the girls that their time was up.

"If the master comes back and catches you, we'll all get a good hiding," I said. "And you must swear on your mother's grave that you won't tell anyone about what you just bought."

"Why?" said Pigtail.

"Because I shouldn't have let you," I said.

"And if you tell other people, they'll all want to come and hold Her Grace, and then I'll have to fight them off, and the master will come looking for you and he'll put you in prison."

The girls went away looking worried, and I fingered the second penny loaf in my pocket. To eat it or not to eat it, that was my dilemma, sir. I doubt if it's one you ever came up against. The thing is, if I ate it, there was no more evidence, and if the girls told tales, then it was their word against mine. But if I ate it, then I wouldn't have it to eat later, and there was no telling how long it would be before my gentleman came back. I decided to save it, at least for the moment.

CHAPTER FOUR

The gentleman had been gone a long time by now, and I was beginning to be anxious for him to come back. I watched the pigs and chickens foraging around in the icy mud and wondered what they could possibly find to eat in that mess.

The street was empty for a while after the girls had gone away, and then a couple of farmers came along, driving some sheep to the butcher's, and then a man in a firewood wagon, which was making heavy weather of the mud, and then a washerwoman with a massive bundle tied up in a grimy sheet. They all looked at the horse and at me, but no one stopped or spoke. Soon after that, though, a man came along, and he took a great interest in me and the horse. I saw him looking at us as he came along the street, and when he drew level, he stopped walking and stood looking.

I didn't like the cut of him, sir, from the time I first laid eyes upon him. When

you live on the street, you get to know
a lot about people. It's a question of sur-
vival. And this man looked shifty to me.
He crossed to my side of the street, as
I had guessed he would, but for a long
time he didn't say a word. He just walked
around the horse, looking her up and
down and over and under and through
and through.

"Who does it belong to?" he said at last. He wasn't that old, but he'd already lost most of his teeth and his speech wasn't all that clear.

"None of your business," I said.

He glared at me so hard that I feared he might aim a blow at me. I knew it wouldn't cost him a second thought. He was no stranger to violence, that fellow.

"How much you asking for it?" he said.

Well, I don't mind telling you, sir, that his question made me stop and think. It hadn't really occurred to me before, despite what I had said to the two girls, but that mare was certainly worth a lot of money.

The man was watching me think, and I wished I could come up with a smart answer, but I was stuck fast in a conflict between the prospect of money and loyalty to the gentleman rider. How much was she worth? That was what I was thinking. An awful lot more than the guinea I'd been promised, that much was certain.

"You're tempted, aren't you?" He stepped closer to me as he said it, and glanced quickly up and down the street.

I wouldn't like you to get the wrong impression, sir. I might be poor but I'm not a thief. All I'm saying is that the prospect of a large amount of money couldn't be passed over without due consideration.

"Indeed I'm not," I said, but I knew my words lacked conviction, and I'm sure old Toothless knew it too.

"Hmm," he said, and went about inspecting the mare all over again, though I very much doubt there was anything about her he hadn't seen on his first go-round.

I looked at her too, with eyes wide open now and with numbers in my mind growing bigger and wilder by the moment. The kind of money the mare might fetch could lift a lad like me out of poverty, sir. Set me up in my own little business, perhaps. Selling pies or muffins around the markets. Or shining boots like yours, sir. I'm sure that you can understand why I was engaged in such a fierce battle with my conscience.

Old Toothless turned to observe a cart that was trundling slowly toward us, and I

turned to look at it too. It was loaded
with turnips and carrots and guarded
by two burly farmers, one in front at
the horse's head and the other behind.
Both of them carried cudgels.

When I turned back, Toothless had disappeared. There hadn't been time for him to get to the end of the street, and I guessed he must have turned into one of the alleyways. My dreams of money had gone with him but I was glad that it was over and that the dreadful temptation had been removed.

CHAPTER FIVE

The farmers stopped to admire the mare. They were both nearly as broad as they were tall, with bulging forearms and heavy shoulders.

One of them had a great head of hair like a haystack but none at all on his chin. The other was practically bald on top but had a gingery

38

beard that grew right down onto his chest. It was so thick, a family of wrens might have been nesting in it. I thought that if you turned his head upside down, he would probably look exactly like his friend.

"Ee, but she's a grand mare," he said, and gave her such a hefty slap on the neck I was afraid she'd fall down.

Haystack gave her a pat on the rump. "Who does she belong to, then?" he said.

You know, sir, it never occurred to me for an instant to mistrust those two. Maybe it was the slow, solid way they moved, or the hard days of work stored up in their muscles, or maybe it was just their eyes, blue as the summer sky and filled with nothing but wonderment.

So I told them about the gentleman and his wild ride into town, and I told them about the promise of the golden guinea, and I told them as well about old Toothless and his sneaky attempts to buy the mare.

"He was wasting his time there, wasn't he?" said Haystack. "Good honest lad like you. He'd get nowhere with that game."

That made me feel good, sir. It almost made me believe that I'd never even considered old Toothless's proposition.

"Never trust a bloke like that, any road," said Wrenbeard. "Sure as not he'd have some sharp lad waiting round the next corner ready to rob the money straight back off you."

Those farmers might have been slow, but they certainly weren't as stupid as they looked. I thought I knew every street trick in the book, but I hadn't thought of that one.

They had a small barrel lashed to the side of their wagon, and since they had stopped, they took the opportunity to pour a drink of water from it. They gave me a dipper of it as well, which was welcome. The mare grew very excited when she got a scent of it.

"She's thirsty, God bless her," said Haystack. When you think of it, she was bound to be, wasn't she, sir, after such a long hard gallop. But it hadn't occurred to me, being as how I'm so ignorant when it comes to horses. There wasn't enough for her in their little barrel, but they had a bucket for their own horse, and Haystack went off with it in search of a pump. When he came back, the mare plunged her nose in until her nostrils were completely under the water.

"You don't often see that," Wrenbeard said. "Most horses keep their nostrils clear."

"Sign of a great heart," said Haystack.

"Is it?" I said.

"So they say," said Haystack.

"So they say," said his friend.

They were completely besotted with her, sir, and very reluctant to move on. Haystack fetched a second bucket of water and Wrenbeard fed her carrots with the tops on and a handful of the oats they had brought for their own mare, though it didn't please her one bit and they had to give her some too. I wanted to keep those two fellows with me forever. They were big and strong and gentle, and they carried their slow, country ways with them wherever they went. Even when another cart came along behind them, they were in no hurry to leave, and it wasn't until the other driver got impatient and began to call them bad names that they eventually took their leave of the mare and me, and picked up their cudgels and went on their way.

CHAPTER SIX

I missed them when they had gone and so did the mare. I swear it, sir. She whinnied after them, and it was the only time during the whole day that she made any kind of sound or took any kind of notice of anyone. But there was someone else who was only too pleased to see the back of those country men. Old Toothless. When I saw him coming back, I had a feeling that he'd been there for a while, waiting for them to move off, hiding down one of those dark little alleys like the gutter rat he was. This time he had someone with him: a stout man in a waistcoat and a pair of very muddy riding breeches. You might think his attire marked him as a gentleman, sir, but I assure you he wasn't. He might have been better dressed, but he was made of the same stuff as Toothless, without a doubt.

And like Toothless had done, he never looked at me at all, but walked around the mare and examined her from every angle you can imagine. And when he'd done that, he strode up to her head, and without any warning or by-your-leave he pulled open her lips to look at her teeth. She didn't like that, sir, not one bit. She threw up her head and backed away into the road, and since I wasn't about to let go of her, she dragged me with her through the mud and the gardyloo.

I protested, sir. I asked them what they meant by assaulting my master's horse in such a way and told them to take themselves off, though not in such polite terms as that.

"Who is this master of yours, then?" the man in the waistcoat asked me. "And why has he abandoned his horse in the middle of a pigsty?"

"He hasn't abandoned her," I said. "He has left her in my keeping. He's sure to return very shortly, and if you know what's good for you, you'll leave well enough alone, because if he were to catch you gawping into her mouth, he wouldn't take kindly to it."

"But he can't think much of her, can he?" he said. "To leave such a fine animal standing in a muck sweat with nothing but a guttersnipe to care for her?"

"I won't have you calling me a gutter-snipe!" I said.

This sent both the men into gales of laughter, and while they were occupied with that I led the mare back to the side of the street. She followed me like a lamb and I rubbed her nose for her so she would know I was pleased.

"I like this lad," said Muddybreeches. "Shall we let him in for a share?"

I don't think Toothless cared much for that idea, but he made no objection and the other one told me his plan.

"I buy and sell a great many horses, and I prefer my dealings to be aboveboard. So I propose to give you thirty shillings for this mare."

"Thirty shillings!" Toothless spat, but Breeches ignored him and continued like this:

"That way you won't go home to your gutter empty-handed, and I can say I bought the horse fair and square. I shall get perhaps seven guineas for her and my friend here will get a share for bringing the matter to my attention. So what do you think of that for an arrangement?"

Thirty shillings was tempting. It was, after all, a full nine shillings more than the guinea I had been promised. And it was all the more tempting when I saw the coin purse come out and heard the very fine jingling sound it made.

"He'll never find you again, lad," said Toothless. "Runt of a thing like you can lose yourself easily enough in a big city like this."

I looked around the street and became aware of a new danger. The two carts had disappeared, leaving deep muddy troughs in their wake. The pigs were already in there, digging in the bottoms with their filthy snouts, but there were no people to be seen anywhere. What was to stop these two crooks from taking the horse anyway and leaving me with nothing? How could I stop them, after all? And that fine gentleman wasn't going to give me a guinea for losing his horse, was he? But still I couldn't agree to it. I was all puffed up and full of my own virtue, after what those two farmers had said about me. Besides, I hadn't forgotten about that smart lad who was probably waiting round the corner. I was resolved not to give up that horse without a fight.

"I won't let you have her," I said. "Not for thirty shillings and not if you were to offer me thirty guineas."

I tightened my grip on the reins, gritted my teeth, and got ready for the blows that I was certain would come next. But yet again the heavens smiled upon me. For the second time that day I felt thunder coming up through my feet, then heard the clatter of hooves approaching along the road, then the jingle of bridles, the delighted calls of a young child, the squawk of a chicken that moved too slowly. Then they came thundering into view: a dozen of the king's soldiers in all their finery. They didn't come as fast as the gentleman on his black horse had done, but it was clear that they had been riding hard because their horses were lathered with sweat and there was so much steam rising from them that it looked as if the soldiers had brought their own cloud along with them, in case they needed rain.

I pulled the mare closer in toward the houses at the side of the street, to give the soldiers more room to pass by, and as I did so, I noticed that Toothless and Muddybreeches had vanished just as

silently as they had first appeared. I con-
fess I wished that I could vanish so easily because, as I'm sure you know, sir,
street beggars and soldiers do not make
natural allies. But I couldn't vanish and
I couldn't prevent them noticing me,
either. Although they had the whole road
to themselves now, they did not pass by.
They stopped, all of them, and stood in
a horseshoe around me, for all the world
like a bristling scarlet fence.

CHAPTER SEVEN

The black mare shifted restlessly and snatched at her bit, and it seemed to me that she was as anxious as I was. The soldiers' horses pawed the ground and tossed their heads impatiently. One of the soldiers got down and handed the reins of his horse to another.

"Whose horse is this?" he asked me.

I swear a dozen different answers jumped into my head, but since I couldn't decide which one to use I let them all get away again, and I said nothing at all. The soldier bent down in front of me until his hard gray eyes were level with mine.

"Do you speak English?" he asked, very slowly.

I would have laughed if I hadn't been so afraid.

"I do, sir," I said.

"I do, Captain," he said.

"I do, *Captain*," I repeated.

"Whose horse is this?" he asked again.

"It belongs to a gentleman," I said, deciding that it was safest to be honest about it. "And he has promised me a guinea if I hold her until he comes back."

The captain straightened up and began

to walk around the mare in a very similar manner to the two crooks. She gave a great sigh, as if she was exhausted with being examined. The captain lifted her feet and peered at her shoes, then he looked at the cloak and at the saddle underneath it.

"She's not for sale, sir," I said.

"*Captain,*" he corrected me.

"She's not for sale, Captain, sir," I said.

"What a shame," he said. "She's a very fine animal."

I was as proud to hear that as if she had been my own, and I found that, despite myself, I was beginning to like this soldier.

"She is indeed, Captain," I said.

"But tell me more about her owner," he said. "What does he look like?"

"As tall as you, sir, Captain, sir. Or very nearly. And he has big black mustaches and long, curly black hair."

"I see," said the captain. "And was he carrying anything with him, do you remember?"

"A saddlebag, Captain. That's all, as far as I remember."

"Good lad," said the captain, and he ruffled my hair just the way the gentleman had done earlier, though I noticed that he wiped his hand on the leg of his breeches afterward, and the gentleman hadn't done that.

He walked back to the scarlet fence and said something to another of the soldiers, and that one dismounted too, and they walked off together to a quiet place farther down the road. They had to go some distance, because quite a crowd had gathered by then, and there was a second horseshoe of curious onlookers crowding round behind the soldiers. Everyone was looking at me, and it felt very pleasant, sir, to have all those eyes upon me and the fine black mare. It made me feel very important.

But it wasn't to last for long. The captain soon came back and gave an order to his troop, and straightaway the soldiers began to clear the crowd and send everyone off about their business. Then the soldiers too, went away, leaving only the captain and the one he had been talking to, and the two horses belonging to them.

The captain came up to me and bent his knees again so he could look me in the eye.

"What's your name, boy?" he said.

I told him, and he went on: "Well, it seems to me that you are a most trustworthy young man."

I nodded earnestly. As I'm sure you can

tell by now, sir, this was very perceptive of the captain.

"Good lad," he went on. "Good lad. And how would you like to do a piece of work for the king?"

"I should like that very much, Captain," I said.

"Good," he said. "And you won't find it difficult at all."

For a moment I dared to imagine myself dressed in scarlet uniform and riding the black mare into a fearsome battle—but it was not that kind of work that the captain had in mind.

"Have you ever heard of a fellow called Dick Turpin?" he asked me.

"Dick Turpin the highwayman?" I said.

"The very same."

Of course I had. Who hadn't? Like every other poor boy in the street, I loved the tales of that famous highwayman. I lurked in the doorways of public houses to listen to his latest exploits, and hid in the shadows of street corners if I ever heard mention of his name, in case there was some new story of his heroics. In my dreams I relived his adventures as he emerged from the forest's edge to waylay another rich man. "Stand and deliver!" That's what he said to them. "Your money or your life!" Dick Turpin was my hero.

I was silent for too long, lost in my thoughts.

"Well?" said the captain. "Have you or haven't you?"

"I have, sir, Captain, sir. I have indeed."

"Well," he said, "I am as sure as I can be that the gentleman who gave you this horse to hold was none other than Dick Turpin himself."

I stared at the captain in disbelief while a hundred new thoughts charged around my head and got in one another's way.

"And this," he went on, straightening up and patting the mare's neck, "is none other than Black Bess."

Chapter Eight

I gasped then, out loud. So the mare really was horse royalty. I hadn't tricked those girls at all. In fact, I had undercharged them!

"Black Bess," I whispered, stroking her nose.

The captain laughed and leaned against her shoulder, one arm thrown loosely over her neck. I have to admit I thought it very cheeky for him to take such a liberty with her, as if she was just some old tinker's nag. But he was a captain of the king's guard, so what could I say? And in any event, I very soon forgot about it in the light of what he said next.

"Dick Turpin waylaid and robbed a mail coach and stole a bag of gold coin that was destined for the Bank of England. When he had gone, the driver unhitched the lead horse and rode ahead, where he happened to encounter me and my men while we were on exercise in the countryside. We were able to pick up Turpin's trail while it was still warm, and it led here. His horse's shoes"—and here he picked up one of Black Bess's feet so he could show me— "have quite an unusual nail pattern, so we had no difficulty tracking him."

I nodded glumly, greatly disliking what I was hearing.

"Perhaps you are mistaken, all the same, Captain," I said. "Perhaps it was some other man's trail you picked up. I don't think the man I saw was Dick Turpin."

He laughed. "Well, perhaps you're right," he said. "But we shall soon find out, shan't we? All we need to do is wait until he returns for his horse, and then we shall know."

"And my part in it, Captain?" I said miserably, although I had already guessed.

"Your part is to do exactly what you are doing now. To stand here with Black Bess and wait for her owner to return. Meanwhile my men and I shall be hiding around the area, and when Mr. Turpin comes, we shall spring out and arrest him."

I was mortified, and still trying to get poor Dick Turpin out of this mess.

"Perhaps it won't work, Captain," I said. "I've heard it said that Dick Turpin can smell a soldier a mile off by the kind of dubbin you all use on your boots."

The captain laughed again. "He will return," he said, "because what would Dick Turpin be without Black Bess?" He patted the mare again. "Where would he find another horse half as fast and as loyal and as brave?"

What was I to do, sir? You can see my predicament. What would you have done? I was so excited, sir, to have met the great Dick Turpin and to be holding his famous horse, but now I was to be bait in a plan to trap him! Worms on a hook, sir, that's what they wanted us to be. Me and poor Black Bess. I looked into her eyes and I knew that she would have hated it as much as me, if only she could understand what was happening.

I thought a lot of thoughts in a very short time, and I'm not proud of all of them. The worst one was about whether

Dick Turpin would have time to hand me my golden guinea before the soldiers closed in on him, and the best one had me dropping Black Bess's reins and walking away from the whole filthy business. But there was another one, which lay somewhere in between, and that was the one I chose to act upon, and it was this: as long as I was there holding Black Bess, there was still a chance that Dick Turpin could get away. If I saw him at a distance, I might shout out to him and warn him of the trap, and he might be able to run and hide. And if he just appeared, creeping up out of the alley the way the two thieves had, I might get him to spring up on Black Bess's back and gallop off before the soldiers had time to move in. These chances were slim, I knew, but they were the best I could come up with.

So there was just one small matter that needed to be dealt with.

"What's in it for me, Captain?" I said. "Dick Turpin promised me a guinea for holding the horse, so I'll be out of pocket, won't I?"

The captain laughed and almost ruffled my hair again, but pulled out at the last minute.

"If we catch Dick Turpin," he said, "you will be well rewarded. Have no fear of it."

He patted the breast of his uniform jacket and I heard the soft music of coinage. And so, although I couldn't do it entirely without shame, I nodded to the captain, and with that nod I agreed to do that piece of work for the king and to play my part in entrapping the man who was my hero and, I liked to think, my friend.

CHAPTER NINE

The captain and his aide mounted up and went away, leaving the dingy old street empty again. I don't know where they hid their horses, and for that matter, I don't know where they hid themselves. I examined every door and window, every rooftop, every shadow in every alley. But I didn't get one glimpse of a scarlet coat or a dubbined boot.

It had been, to say the least, a very

strange day, as I'm sure you understand. I had never in my life been offered so much money by so many people, and yet I still hadn't seen a penny of it. I couldn't decide whether I had made the right decisions, and all the events of the day kept racing round and round in my mind.

Bess wasn't happy, either. She was restless, looking this way and that and tugging on the reins as if she wanted to drag me off along the street. I held on tight and kept her there. I stroked her on the nose to try and calm her, but she shook her head and shoved me so hard in the chest that I nearly fell over.

"There, there, Bess," I said. "It's all right." But she wouldn't look at me now, and I came to believe that she knew exactly what was going on and wanted no part in the unsavory plan. I kept wishing that I had no part in it either, sir, but I could not see a way out of it now. I was surrounded by soldiers, and if I tried to run away, I might myself be arrested as a criminal. Several more times Bess pushed me hard with her nose against my chest, and after a while I realized what the problem was. I had lost track of the time we had been standing there together, but it must have been several hours. The few nibbles that Wrenbeard had given the mare were long forgotten by now, and the poor thing must have been ravenous again.

You know something, sir? If I had been with another lad or girl that day, nothing could have induced me to share what I had with them. I had grown up too hard, I suppose, and when you get as low down as me, then it's every man for himself, so to speak. I would have sneaked away somewhere quiet where I could be on my own and eat the penny loaf I'd saved in my pocket, and no one else would have got so much as a sniff of it.

So why on earth should a horse be any different? I can't answer that, sir, but I shared my last bit of bread with that mare, and that is God's honest truth. It didn't make any sense, either. That loaf was a meal for me, and it was barely a mouthful for her, but all the same she had her share, and more than her share, and do you know, I got nearly as much pleasure from watching her eat as I did from eating myself.

I'm told the king takes two hours over his dinner every day, but I can't imagine that. I never even saw so much food in one place as would take the king and his company two hours to eat. I think of that as heaven. Two hours with nothing else to do but eat. The mare and I scoffed the bread in two minutes, sir, or less. And after that, we were back to the plain old waiting again.

I notice you have a fine pair of boots, sir, and I doubt you ever knew what it's like to lose all the feeling in your feet, but it's a thing I wouldn't wish on my worst enemy. On the coldest days it happens, and it's very peculiar. You'd know you were standing up, but you wouldn't have any idea what you were standing on. It might be cobbles and it might be mud and you might be standing in water up to your ankles, but unless you took the trouble to look, you'd have no idea.

And it was beginning to happen to me now, standing there waiting. Usually when it happens, I walk around until my feet warm up or I forget about them, but on this occasion, of course, there was nowhere for me to go. I had no choice but to put up with it.

Dusk began to fall, the grim, early dusk of midwinter, and the street became busy with people returning from their day's work and setting about their household business. Men and women passed up and down with buckets, on their way to and from the pump. Children were sent out into the street to play while their suppers were cooked, and some of them gathered round to look at Bess. One stupid boy thought it funny to throw stones at her. I didn't dare tell him who she belonged to, but I stopped him by returning one of his missiles, and hard enough for it to sting.

As dusk gave way to darkness, the children were sent to round up the pigs and the chickens, and then everyone disappeared inside and closed the doors and the shutters. I don't suppose it was so warm inside those houses, but from where I was standing it looked it. The smells of cooking drove me to distraction. Candlelight leaked through the door and window frames, and wood smoke spilled from chimneys. It seemed so unfair, sir, that I had no family to go to and no hearth to thaw my frozen toes.

I thought about Dick Turpin and wondered where he was. Somewhere warm, no doubt. Spending his money and eating his fill, his high boots steaming before some hearty fire.

The brief pat and a promise that he had given me began to feel like less of a privilege in the light of that understanding. Perhaps he wasn't such a kind man if he was prepared to leave me in my bare feet in the coming darkness, with the ice on the mud puddles beginning to freeze over again.

Or perhaps it was true, what they said about him. Perhaps he had tried to come and get Black Bess and give me my guinea, but he'd got a whiff of the dubbin on the soldiers' boots and had turned away, smelling the trap we had laid for him.

I was looking at a long night ahead of me in the bitter cold, and I began to wish that it had never been my misfortune to meet Dick Turpin and Black Bess.

CHAPTER TEN

They came in the night, sir, as I might have guessed they would, Toothless and his portly friend. I never saw or heard them coming at all. They just appeared, sneaking silently up the alley behind me.

My first thought when I saw them was to take their thirty shillings and run. Even if the soldiers caught me, I'd be better off than I would be standing there and perishing in the cold. But they never offered it this time. They just pushed me into the mud and made off with the horse.

I'm not very big, sir, as you can see, but I can make a big noise if I choose to, and I did so then. The door of the nearest house opened, but I was already running after the men and Black Bess. I needn't have, though. Because the soldiers had also appeared, as if from nowhere, and they were everywhere around us in the dark, blocking every mouth of every alley. The men tried to make a run for it, but they hadn't a hope. They were collared in no time and brought back to my corner, and pushed against the wall. There was plenty of light by this time, because the commotion had caused half the people

in the street to open their doors. And the other half, I suppose, to bolt them more securely.

"But the horse is mine," Muddybreeches was saying. "That urchin stole her from me."

"Is that true, lad?" said the captain, strolling in from one of the alleyways. "Is this the man who asked you to look after his horse?"

I'm good at thinking on my feet, sir. You have to be if you live on your wits, like I do. But on that occasion I didn't think fast enough. It could all have been over, you see. If I had said yes, there could have been an end to it all.

"But he promised me a guinea and now he has to give it to me" is what I should have said. Muddybreeches would gladly have given me a guinea to get off the hook, and he would have got himself a great bargain. As for me, I could have taken myself off to the nearest pie shop and got myself a bellyful of steak and kidney.

But there was an even better outcome to that particular plan, and it was this. If I named Muddybreeches as the owner of the horse, then the soldiers would stop watching for Dick Turpin, wouldn't they? So when he did come back for Black Bess, he would be disappointed, of course, and he would think that I had let him down, and that would be very unfortunate if it were to happen that I encountered him again someday. But what matters is that he would have his freedom, and he could go about his business on the highways. It was, in fact, the perfect solution to everyone's problems.

But did I say yes?

No. I said no.

Two such small words, sir, but what a big difference between them. I said no, and the soldiers laid hands on the two men instantly, as if they were following my personal orders. Such a sense of power that gave me, but it didn't last for long. Muddybreeches spat at me as they took him away, which goes to prove that he was no gentleman, despite his waistcoat and his boots.

Three of the soldiers went with the men and the rest vanished back to wherever they had been hiding before. Only the captain remained behind, and he clapped me on the shoulder and said:

"Back to your post, young man."

My heart sank at the thought of more standing around in the darkness and the cold. But what could I do? I led the mare back to our station and adjusted the cloak on her back. It was wonderfully warm beneath it, where the heavy woolen cloth trapped the heat from her body, and I envied her and wondered how it was that a beast could be so well provided for and comfortable when I was so miserable and cold. But that was my lot, sir, and I was well accustomed to suffering it, so I pulled my tattered old coat around me as tight as I could and stamped my icy feet up and down on the ground.

I don't know how long we stood like that, with the mare moving her weight from one hind leg to the other and myself leaning against the wall and doing the same thing. I know there are some people who take pleasure from the hours of darkness, but I'm not one of them. It's during the night that I remember my life at home before my mother died, and when there is nothing to look at, it's difficult to keep your mind away from dwelling on the bad things that happen. I measure my days by the passage of the sun through the sky and by the length of the roads and streets I travel, but I have no way of measuring the hours of darkness, so I have no idea what time of night it was when Black Bess grew tired of standing and, very carefully, laid herself down on her belly.

And now that she no longer towered over me, I saw a way in which we could share Dick Turpin's cloak and both stay warm beneath it. I had never sat astride a horse before, but with her back now so close to the ground, it didn't seem to me to be a very great risk to take when the return was the promise of such warmth.

Very slowly and quietly, taking care not to alarm the mare, I put the reins back over her head and climbed into the saddle. She sighed in the darkness but she made no other objection. I pushed myself to the very back of the saddle, then leaned forward over her withers. The cloak came over my back and up to my neck, but a draft still came in beneath it, so I felt along the collar until I found the buckle and strap, and I fastened them beneath my chin.

The cloth still held a rank smell from the mare's dried sweat, but it held the heat from her body as well, and I began to warm up so fast that I got pains in my hands and feet. But there was pleasure too, sir: the pure delight of being warm, and even before the pains had faded away I had drifted off into sleep, with my cheek resting on the mare's thick mane.

CHAPTER ELEVEN

I woke to the alarming sensation of the mare clambering to her feet beneath me. It was so dark that I thought my eyes were gummed together, as they often are when I wake up in the mornings, but then I caught a glimpse of a few stars above the rooftops, and I knew it was still the dead of night.

"Off you get, lad. It's all over."

It was the captain's voice, and now I could make out his form in the street beside me. But I was looking down at him instead of up, because I was sitting high on the mare's back.

"What's all over?" I said. "What's happening?"

"Two constables caught Dick Turpin yesterday afternoon. The report of it has only just reached us."

He sounded very cross. I wondered whose fault it was that he and his men had stood for half the night in the freezing cold, waiting to catch a man who had already been caught.

"So down you get, and off home with you."

But I wasn't ready to get down, and in any case I had no home to go to. And there was another thing.

"What about my payment?" I said.

"Oh, hang your payment," said the

captain, and he reached up to take hold of my arm and pull me down.

But I wasn't coming down. My heart filled with fury at the way I had been used. Did he really think that he could treat me like that? Keep me standing around all day and night and then just send me on my way without so much as a six- pence? I yanked my arm away and kicked out at him as hard as I could. I missed him by a mile, but as my leg returned, my heel slammed hard into Black Bess's flank. And, noblest of mares, she didn't need to be asked twice. She spun away from my heel and lit out along the street as though the devil was after her. Lord knows how I stayed in the saddle, but now that we were moving I clung onto her mane as tight as I could, knowing that my life might very well depend upon it.

It's a good thing that horses see better in the dark than people do, because I had no idea where we were going. Black Bess did, though, and her feet were sure and safe as she splashed through the muck and ice. Soon I could tell by the smell of the air that we had left the city behind and entered the countryside beyond.

Still the mare galloped on, showing no sign of tiring. I very much wished she would.

I had no idea whether the soldiers were in pursuit, but I had another serious problem, which might prove even more dangerous to me than them. The cloak, Dick Turpin's wonderful warm black cloak, was streaming out behind me just as it had streamed behind him when he galloped into town the previous day.

How he arranged it I have no idea, but I am sure it wasn't throttling him the way it was now throttling me. And because I was no rider I didn't dare lift a hand from my grip on the mare's mane, in case I tumbled off the side onto the unseen road rushing past beneath us. The reins were there somewhere, flapping against her neck and the backs of my hands, but it was going to require a huge leap of faith for me to try and grab them.

Unless I did, though, I would be strangled by Dick Turpin's cloak, and it seemed like a particularly stupid way to die, given all that I had gone through. So I took one hand from Black Bess's mane and groped about in the wind that was whistling past her neck, until I felt the cold, greasy leather of the rein, and clutched at it.

Being a rider yourself, sir—and a fine one, I dare say—you will know better than to haul on one rein while leaving the other to dangle free. Had I been stronger it is likely that I would have brought Black Bess down, and myself along with her in a heap in the mud. But as it was, I only succeeded in turning her off the road and into a grove of trees, where she was obliged to come to a very rapid stop. Naturally I went straight over her head and landed in a bramble patch, with the black cloak settling on top of me.

And I was still trying to disentangle myself from that muddle when I heard the thunder of hooves on the road behind us, as the king's captain and his troop of soldiers went flying past.

Yet again trying to capture someone who wasn't there.

CHAPTER TWELVE

So that's my story, sir. And I don't know how you would feel about it, but it seems to me that the mare is rightfully mine. She was left in my care, you see, and the man who owned her is due to be hanged very shortly, as I'm sure you will have heard, and he has no use for her now.

It did cross my mind to take up where Dick Turpin left off, and to pursue the highwayman's trade. But I'm small, sir, as you can see, and I can't imagine coachmen or travelers paying much attention to me, especially since Dick Turpin took his saddlebag with him and left me with no pistol.

So that's why I'm offering her for sale, sir, because I'm a poor city lad and can't afford to keep a horse. The cloak too, if you were interested, though it wouldn't come cheap because of its fascinating history.

Yes, I've heard the same thing myself, sir; that there are other people out there

claiming to be in possession of Black Bess and offering her for sale. All I can say to that is: see for yourself. You don't need me to point out what a fine animal you're looking at.

Well, naturally she looks a bit tired. Wouldn't you, sir, if you'd been through what she has? And of course a new set of shoes would make her feet look a lot tidier. Well, maybe she could use a bit of a trim around the fetlocks, but really, sir, to call her a carthorse is most unfair.

No, no. I couldn't take that for her. That's an insult. She's worth ten times that. This is Black Bess you're looking at, sir, not just any old nag.

I see. Well, suit yourself, sir. No charge

for looking. And there are plenty more horsemen out there that will leap at the chance of buying the one and only Black Bess. I'll have no trouble selling her, will I, Bess? No trouble at all.

THE END